D0119052

Ernest and the BIG Itch

Ernest and the BIG Itch is part of the Ernest Series®.

Barnesyard Books and Ernest are trademarks of Barnesyard Books, Inc.

Book design by Christine Wolstenholme

Published by Barnesyard Books, Sergeantsville, NJ 08557
www.barnesyardbooks.com

Printed in China

Library of Congress Catalog Card Number: 2001 130674

ISBN 0-9674681-2-4

Ernest and the BIG Itch

by Laura T. Barnes

Illustrated by Carol A. Camburn

Sergeantsville, NJ 08557 • www.barnesyardbooks.com

For Jeff – my best friend and husband

– L.T.B.

For James

– C.A.C.

Chipper woke up slowly, admiring his surroundings.
He loved his birdhouse and its view of the morning sunrise over the barnyard.

"Ah, what a great morning," thought Chipper. "I have a feeling it's going to be a beautiful day.
I can see the sun just starting to rise."

Chipper hopped back
inside to wake up his little sister.
"Wake up, Sis," he sang. "Wake up and watch the morning sunrise with me."

Sis opened her sleepy eyes and saw Chipper. He had a big, wide smile.
"Will you ever get tired of seeing the sunrise?" she giggled at her brother.

"No," chimed Chipper. "I love the early morning sky. It's so colorful. Look, it's
yellow with a little bit of orange starting to peek through. Come on. Get up and
watch it with me."

Sis crawled out of bed and stretched her wings.

She looked out and agreed, "Yes, you're right Chipper. It is pretty."

As they watched the sunrise, they suddenly felt a big jolt.
The jolt was so big they were both tossed to the other end of their birdhouse.

"What, what was that?" stuttered a surprised Chipper. And before he could stand up, he felt another jolt. Followed by another. And another!

Soon their whole house was rattling and shaking. Straw scattered everywhere. Twigs tumbled across the room.

"What's happening?" questioned Sis as her nest started to crumble. Then it fell completely apart. Everything in their home was being tossed in every direction.

"What on earth…?" sobbed Sis.

"That's it! I think it's an *earth*quake!" exclaimed Chipper.

Sis cried, "An earthquake? Oh no!"

"Calm down and wait here," said Chipper. "I'm going to look outside."

Chipper slowly made his way to the door. He carefully crept out onto the ledge and looked around. Strangely, he did not see anything trembling.

Chipper looked out at the pasture and saw that the horses were calmly grazing.

He looked up at the trees and saw the branches were not shaking.

He looked toward the stream. It was flowing smoothly.

Chipper was very puzzled. His house was still shaking. He held on tightly to keep his balance. "What on earth? Is this really an earthquake?" he wondered.

Then slowly, he looked down. He looked directly down to the ground. To his surprise he saw a furry little donkey. Looking closer, he saw it was a *very* tiny miniature donkey.

The little donkey was leaning against the pole that held their birdhouse. He was rubbing against the pole. Amazed, Chipper watched as the furry, little donkey rubbed up-and-down and to-and-fro.

Chipper grinned. He realized that the donkey had an itch. For such a little donkey he had a *BIG* itch. He was using the pole to scratch his back.

Chipper chuckled to his sister, "Don't worry, it is not an earthquake. It's not an earthquake at all! It's only a tiny donkey rubbing against the pole that holds our birdhouse. I will talk to him. I'll see if he can find some place else to scratch his itch."

Chipper flew outside. "Excuse me little donkey.
Would you be so kind as to stop rubbing against this pole?" asked Chipper.

Startled, the little donkey looked at the bird. "Oh – hi!" said the donkey. "I'm Ernest!"

"Chipper. My name is Chipper. I live up there. In the house on top of the pole.
Your scratching is making my house rattle and shake. Twigs and branches have scattered everywhere."

"Oh, sorry," said Ernest. "I didn't know that I was bothering you. But you see I have this itch. A *BIG* itch. This pole is just perfect for me to scratch it."

"Maybe we can find some place else for you to scratch your itch," said Chipper. "How about the fence over there?"

Ernest shook his head. "No, no. The bottom rail of the fence is too low and the top rail is too high. The fence will not do."

Chipper wanted his house to stop rattling so he tried to come up with a new idea to help Ernest.
"How about scratching your itch against that ladder?" asked Chipper.

Ernest walked over to the ladder. "No, no, the ladder is not good for scratching," said Ernest.
"It won't work. The ladder will fall down if I try to rub against it."

"Let's see," said Chipper looking around the barnyard for another idea.
He knew they needed to find a new place for Ernest to scratch his itch. "Oh, I know, I know.
How about this fine tree over here? Follow me."

Chipper landed on the branch of a nearby tree. "Look, Ernest, this tree is perfect to scratch your itch," said Chipper.

"You're silly! Look how tall those branches are. I can't reach them, I'm way too short," laughed Ernest.

"No, no. Not the branches Ernest! The trunk of the tree! It's better than the pole that holds our house. It has nice, thick, rough bark. This will be perfect to scratch your itch," explained Chipper.

Ernest walked over to the tree. The tree trunk did have nice coarse bark and
the branches would shade him from the sun. Yes, it looked like the perfect place to scratch his itch.

He leaned against the tree and started moving up-and-down and to-and-fro.

"Ahh," said Ernest. "This is just perfect. *Yea for me!*"

"I won't need to use your birdhouse to scratch my itch anymore.
This tree is better! How can I ever thank you?" asked Ernest.

"No, no, don't thank me," said Chipper.
"We helped each other come up with an answer that makes us *both* happy!"

But Ernest did want to thank his new friend. He left the tree and went to the pile of hay by the fence. He took a big mouthful of hay and walked over to Chipper's birdhouse.

"Here, Chipper," offered Ernest. "Let me help clean the mess that I made when I shook your birdhouse. Use my hay to help fluff up your nests and spruce up your home."

Chipper smiled and gladly took the hay into his birdhouse.

Chipper and his sister spent
the day cleaning up their home.
At last the birdhouse was clean
again. They smiled at their fluffy
new nests.

What a special day it had been. Chipper helped Ernest find a
better place to scratch his itch. And, thanks to the hay from Ernest, Chipper's home
looked better than before.

Chipper and Sis went back outside to join Ernest.

Everyone gathered by the tree. They were just in time to see the sun go down.
The new friends watched the beautiful sunset together and enjoyed the end to a great day.